PENROD'S PARTY

Mary Blount Christian
Pictures by S. D. Schindler

Ready-to-Read®

Macmillan Publishing Company
New York
Collier Macmillan Publishers
London

Macmillan Publishing Company
866 Third Avenue, New York, NY 10022
Collier Macmillan Canada, Inc.
Printed and bound in Singapore
First American Edition

10 9 8 7 6 5 4 3 2 1

The text of this book is set in 18 point Century Expanded.
The illustrations are rendered in pen-and-ink and watercolor.
READY-TO-READ is a registered trademark of Macmillan, Inc.

Library of Congress Cataloging-in-Publication Data
Christian, Mary Blount.
Penrod's party/Mary Blount Christian;
pictures by S.D. Schindler. — 1st ed.
p. cm. — (Ready-to-read)
Summary: Presents the amusing adventures of two friends,
Griswold Bear and Penrod Porcupine.
ISBN 0-02-718525-7
[1. Bears — Fiction. 2. Porcupines — Fiction. 3. Friendship —
Fiction.] I. Schindler, S.D., ill. II. Title. III. Series.
PZ7.C4528Pf 1990 [E] — dc20 89-37203 CIP AC

CONTENTS

See Here, Penrod!   4

Bumpity Bump   15

Those Are the Breaks   26

Penrod's Party   35

SEE HERE, PENROD!

Griswold Bear waved to his friend,
Penrod Porcupine.

"Where have you been?"
Penrod asked.

"At the library,"
Griswold said.
"Where have *you* been?"

"I have been at home,"
Penrod said.

"Now I am going
to Swinton Pig's Barber Shop.
I need a quill cut."
Penrod ran his fingers
through his quills.

"Yes, they are long,"
Griswold said.
"They nearly cover your eyes."

Griswold pulled a book
from his bookbag.
He handed it to Penrod.
"I got this at the library.
I have read it two times.
I just love the story.
Here, you may read it.
You will love it, too."

Penrod shook his head.
His quills flopped in his face.
He handed back the book.
"I cannot read it," he said.
"You read it to me."

Griswold gasped.

"You do not know how to read?
You should learn to read.
It is fun."

Penrod frowned.

"Of course I can read!
I can read when I can see,
that is."

"You cannot see the words?
Then you must visit
Dr. Duck," Griswold said.
"He will help you see the words."

"I do not like to go to doctors,"
Penrod said.
"But I will visit Dr. Duck
if you will go with me."

"I will go with you,"
Griswold said.
"What are friends for?"

"But first we must stop
at Swinton Pig's,"
Penrod said.

"Fine," Griswold said.

They went to the barber shop.

Swinton Pig cut Penrod's quills.

Griswold read his book again.

Then the two friends
went to Dr. Duck's office.
Dr. Duck pointed
to an eye chart.
"Read the bottom line,"
he told Penrod.

"I cannot read the bottom line,"
Penrod said.

Griswold leaned forward.
He peered at the chart.
"Poor Penrod," he said.
"He needs glasses."

"Read the middle line,"
Dr. Duck told Penrod.

"I cannot read the middle line,"
Penrod said.

Griswold leaned forward.
He squinted at the chart.
"Poor, dear Penrod," he said.

"Read the top line,"
Dr. Duck told Penrod.

"I cannot read the top line,"
Penrod said.

Griswold walked close
to the chart and looked.
"My poor, dear Penrod.
That is the biggest line of all.
He cannot see the letters
on the eye chart."

"Oh!" Penrod said.
"I can *see* the *letters*
 on the eye chart.
 They are P B Q R O,
 V W U M Q, and I P R O B.
 But Dr. Duck told me
 to *read* the *lines*.
 I do not know what words
 the letters spell.
 So I cannot *read* them."

"Ha!" Griswold said.

"You *do* need glasses!
The lines say
B R O P Q,
U W V N O,
and T U V B R.
And just this morning,
you could not see my book!"

"That was before
I got my quill cut,"
Penrod said.

"I could not *see*
because my quills were in my eyes."

Dr. Duck brought some glasses.
"Wear these glasses
   when you read," he said.
   He gave the glasses to Griswold.

"Do not worry," Penrod said.
"Now that my quills are short,
   I will read to *you*!"

"*Grrrrr*!" Griswold said.

BUMPITY BUMP

Griswold rode up and down
on his shiny, new red bike.
He rang the bell.
Rrrrring!
He sounded the horn.
Beep! Beep!
He waved to Penrod.

Griswold did a wheelie.
Then he skidded to a stop
in front of Penrod's.
"See my shiny new bike?"
he said.
"It has a basket
to carry things in.
It has a light
to use at night.
I got it at Ebenezer Weasel's
Hardware Store."

"I wish I could ride a bike,"
Penrod said.
"But I do not know how."

"I will show you,"
Griswold said.
He sped up the street,
then down again.
He skidded to a stop.

"That looks easy," Penrod said.
"Let me try."
Penrod climbed onto the bike.
He pushed off.
The front wheel wobbled.
Bumpity bump!
He ran into a tree.
Some shiny red paint
peeled away.

"Come back with my bike!"
Griswold yelled.
"You must point the front wheel
where you want to go."

"Do not worry!" Penrod said.
"I will point the wheel this time."
He pointed the wheel.
But he pedaled too slowly.
Bumpity bump!
Over the bike went,
into a fence.
The new bell would not ring.

"You must point the wheel
and pedal faster,"
Griswold told Penrod.
"Come back here with my bike!"

18

"Do not worry!" Penrod called.
"I will point the wheel
and pedal faster."

Bumpity bump!
The bike rolled into the ditch.
Penrod squeezed the horn.
Instead of *beep, beep,*
it went *blah.*

Griswold jumped up and down.

"You must point the wheel.

You must pedal faster.

And you *must not shut your eyes!*"

Griswold said.

"*Grrrrr!*"

"I will point the wheel.

I will·pedal faster.

I will open my eyes,"

Penrod said.

"Do not worry!"

Then he disappeared

around the corner.

Griswold waited.

He waited and waited.

Finally Penrod came back
around the other corner.

The bike's basket hung lopsided.

The night-light was smashed.

More red paint peeled away.

Griswold cried,

"My bike!

My beautiful, shiny, new bike!"

Penrod looked at the bike.

"Oh, dear," he said.

"I did scratch it up a bit."

"A bit," Griswold said.

"Grrrrr!"

"Do not worry," Penrod said.

"I will buy you a new bike.

It is only fair."

"Only fair," Griswold said.

"And you can have this bike."

Penrod went to Ebenezer Weasel's
Hardware Store.
Griswold stayed home.
He fixed the old bike
for Penrod.

Soon Penrod came back.
He had a big, big box.
"Oh, boy!" Griswold said.
"My new, new bike!"

Penrod tore open the box.

He pulled out the new bike.

"See?" Penrod said.

"It is shiny and red,
just like the first one.

It has a bell."

Rrrrrring!

"It has a horn."

Beep! Beep!

"It has a basket
to carry things in.

And it has a light
to use at night.

It is just right!"

Penrod smiled happily.

Griswold climbed onto the bike.

It was too small.

"Just right for *you*!" he said.

"*Grrrrr!*"

THOSE ARE THE BREAKS

Griswold went to Penrod's.
Balder and Harry Bear Cub
answered the door.
"We were just leaving,"
Balder said.
"Hello and good-bye,"
Harry said.

Griswold went inside.

"Oh, dear!" he said.

Penrod was wrapped
in bandages
from his head to his toes.

"My poor, dear friend!"
Griswold said.

"When did this happen?"

"Just now," Penrod said.

"Do not move," Griswold said.

"I will make you
a nice cup of tea."

"Why, thank you, Griswold,"
Penrod said.
"I will not move."

Griswold went into the kitchen.
He made some tea.
He took it to Penrod.

Griswold plumped the pillows.
"Is there anything else
I can do for you?" he asked.

"Well," Penrod said.
"I do see dust on the lamp."

Griswold dusted the lamp.

"And my rugs look dirty,"
  Penrod said.

Griswold vacuumed the rugs.

"I should go to the grocer's,"
  Penrod said.
"I have nothing for supper."

"I will go to the grocer's,"
  Griswold said.
"I will fix your supper,
  dear friend.
  You must rest."

"Why, thank you," Penrod said.
"I will not move."

Griswold hurried to the grocer's.
Cyrena Hyena and Rhoda Horse
were there, too.
Griswold told them about Penrod.
"I will make him some soup.
Then he will feel better,"
he said.

"I will bake him some bread,"
Cyrena said.

"I will make a pie,"
Rhoda said.

They agreed to meet
at Griswold's house.

Griswold bought carrots,
peas, potatoes, and leeks.
He hurried home.
He made soup.

Cyrena and Rhoda
stopped at Griswold's.
They walked together
to Penrod's house.

"Come in," Penrod said.
"What a nice surprise."
He did not have one bandage on.

"Penrod!" Griswold said.
"Only hours ago
  you were hurt!
  I made you tea."

"It was delicious,"
  Penrod said.
"But I was not hurt."

"You were bandaged
  from head to toe.
  I dusted and vacuumed
  for you."

"I was bandaged
  from head to toe,"
  Penrod said.
"But I was not hurt."

"We three cooked your supper,"
  Griswold said.
"Why were you bandaged
  from head to toe
  if you were not hurt?"

"Balder and Harry must earn
  their first-aid badges,"
  Penrod said.
"I let them practice on me."

"*Grrrrr!*" Griswold said.

The four friends ate piping hot
soup, bread, and pie.

"Today you made tea for me,"
  Penrod told Griswold.
"You dusted and vacuumed.
  You made soup, too."

"Yes," Griswold grumbled.
"What do you have to say
  about that?"

"I. *thank* you, kind Griswold,"
  Penrod said.
"But you *did* forget
  to do the dishes."

"*Grrrrr!*"

PENROD'S PARTY

Griswold answered the door.

It was Penrod.

"May I borrow your punch bowl?"
he asked.

Griswold got the punch bowl.

Penrod's pocket bulged.

"What is in there?" Griswold asked.

"Party invitations," Penrod said.

"I am going to mail them."

Griswold watched
for the mail every day.
He got bills.
He got ads.
But he did not get an invitation
to Penrod's party.

Griswold heard a knock.
It was Penrod again.
"May I borrow your tablecloth?"
he asked.
Griswold got the tablecloth.

"When is your party?"
Griswold asked.

"The twelfth," Penrod said.
"Everybody is coming."

Griswold grumbled to himself.
Not *everybody*.

"That reminds me," Penrod said.
"If it were your party,
what would you serve?"

"Spinach and broccoli,"
Griswold said.
Let them eat *ikky* stuff!
Let them have an awful time.

"No cake?" Penrod said.

"Cauliflower cake," Griswold said.

"Hmmm," Penrod said.
"And ice cream?"

"Onion ice cream," Griswold said.

"Onion?" Penrod asked.
"Do you think they would like that?"

"It is *my* favorite,"
  Griswold said.
  Let them hate the food.
  What did *he* care?

Penrod thanked Griswold
for his suggestions.
He left.

Griswold chuckled.

The guests would be miserable.

Why should he worry?

He was not even invited.

Penrod returned to Griswold's.

"I am giving a present
to a dear friend," he said.

"What do you suggest?"

Griswold hid a smile.

"Underwear," he said.

"Are you sure?" Penrod asked.

"Sure," Griswold said.
"Underwear—and plenty of socks.
I just *love* to get underwear.
And ties and handkerchiefs."

Penrod thanked him and left.
Griswold snickered.
They would have awful food
and awful gifts.
It would be a terrible party
without him!

The twelfth arrived.

Griswold went jogging.

He saw Cyrena Hyena

and Rhoda Horse.

They had big bags of cauliflower.

"We are making a cake," they said.

Then they hurried away.

"Ha," Griswold said.

His trick was working.

Then Griswold saw

Balder and Harry with spinach,

broccoli, and onions.

Griswold laughed.

The party would be terrible.

The afternoon was dark and rainy.

"What a dreary day!"

Griswold said.

Then he smiled.

"A perfect day

for Penrod's party."

He watched through his window.

Cyrena and Rhoda passed by.

Balder and Harry passed by.

Swinton Pig passed by.

Dr. Duck passed by.

They all went into Penrod's.

The telephone rang.

It was Penrod.

"Do you have napkins
I can borrow?" he asked.

"You have my punch bowl,"
Griswold said.
"You have my tablecloth.
You have all my friends.
Of course you should have
my napkins," he said.

"Thank you, Griswold,"
Penrod said. He giggled.
"Will you bring them over?"

"*Grrrrr*!" Griswold said.

"Certainly. It is raining.
I would not want
my good friend
to get wet!"
He grabbed the napkins
and went to Penrod's.

The door was open.
He went inside.
"Surprise!" everyone yelled.
"Happy birthday, Griswold!"

"But —" Griswold said.

His mouth fell open.

"We have your favorite things,"
Penrod said.

"Onion ice cream
and cauliflower cake.
We have broccoli and spinach, too."

"Oh!" Griswold said.

"And those presents?"

"Underwear, socks, handkerchiefs,
and ties," Penrod said.

"Just as you wanted.
Aren't you surprised?"

"I am," Griswold said.
"My birthday is *next* month!"

"Oh!" Penrod said.
"Then I am surprised, too!
  Do not worry.
  We will give you another party
  next month."

  Griswold grinned.
"Can we have chocolate cake
  and raspberry ice cream then?"

"Oh, yes!" Penrod said.
"We would all like that better."

"Yes!" everyone shouted.

"And no underwear or socks?"
Griswold asked.

"No underwear or socks,"
Penrod said.

The friends decided to go
to the ice-cream parlor.
They ordered their favorite flavors.
Then they sang
"Happy No Birthday."

"Now your party will not
  be a surprise,"
  Penrod told Griswold.

"Do not worry,"
  Griswold said to Penrod.
"You will always
  be full of surprises!"